First published in the United States of America in 2009 by Walker Publishing Company, Inc.
Visit Walker & Company's Web site at www.walkeryoungreaders.com

For information about permission to reproduce selections from this book, write to
Permissions, Walker & Company, 175 Fifth Avenue, New York, New York 10010

Library of Congress Cataloging-in-Publication Data
Bazer, Gina.
Now hiring : White House dog / Gina Bazer & Renanah Lehner ; illustrations by Andrew Day.
p.   cm.
Summary: While their parents—the President and the First Lady—prepare for a big,
fancy dinner, two little sisters conduct secret dog interviews to find the perfect pet.
ISBN-13: 978-0-8027-8486-5 • ISBN-10: 0-8027-8486-0 (hardcover)
ISBN-13: 978-0-8027-8487-2 • ISBN-10: 0-8027-8487-9 (reinforced)
[1. Dogs—Fiction. 2. Sisters—Fiction. 3. Presidents—Family—Fiction. 4. White House (Washington, D.C.)—Fiction.
5. African Americans—Fiction. 6. Youths' art.] I. Lehner, Renanah. II. Day, Andrew, ill. III. Title.
PZ7.B3479No 2009   [E]—dc22   2009000853

Art created using pencil, ink, and watercolor • Typeset in Elroy • Book design by Donna Mark

Printed in the U.S.A. by Worzalla
2 4 6 8 10 9 7 5 3 1 (hardcover)
2 4 6 8 10 9 7 5 3 1 (reinforced)

YUKI

FALA

CHECKERS

NOW HIRING: WHITE HOUSE DOG

Gina Bazer AND Renanah Lehner
ILLUSTRATED BY Andrew Day

Walker & Company New York

For Saul and Mark. And for Danielle, dear friend and conspirator. —G. B.

For Randy and our girls, Hannah and Lilah. For D. J. S., the best of the best. —R. K. L.

To my father, who is a constant inspiration to me. —A. D.

One spring day in the most important house in the land, two sisters pressed their noses to a window and waited for a dog.

"Very soon," Mom and Dad had said—but that was in January. Now it was April, and the girls were taking matters into their own hands.

That morning they brought markers to Dad's office, made a sign—Now Hiring: White House Dog—and stuck it in the White House lawn.

"All the dogs on Pennsylvania Avenue will see it," the older sister said.

"But will any want to be our dog?" asked the younger sister.

With their noses to the window, they waited.
Oh, how they longed for a woof, growl, or bark.

Instead, they got a DING-DONG!

"Who could that be?" their mom cried from
upstairs. "The party doesn't start for another
hour!" Their parents were expecting 100 very
important guests for dinner that night—none of
them dogs.

"Somebody, anybody, please answer the door!"

"We'll get it," said the girls, and off they ran.

The first job applicant stood groomed and ready.

"*Yip! Yip! Yip!* My name is Minnie.
Do you mind a dog that's skinny?
I don't really like to play,
But I'll sit on your lap all day.
My kind of fun is a shopping run.
A boa? A sweater? No matter the weather.
What do you think? Do you like pink?"

It worked—a dog was at their door!
Could this be the one for them?
"Stay here," the older sister said. "We'll be right back."

"Is it the Queen of England?" their mom
called from above.

"No, it's not the Queen of England,"
the girls called back.

Before they could invite their guest
inside—DING-DONG!

A shaggy dog panted for their
attention.

"Pleased to meet ya. The name is Stan.
I'm the leader of this furry band.
I'll round you up and lead you home.
I'd never leave you loose to roam.
I've got top-notch skills in organization.
I'll keep you prepared for any situation."

Now the sisters were confused. Which dog should come inside?

"Please stay," the older sister said. "We'll be right back."

"Is it the Grand Duke of Luxembourg?" their dad asked, strolling past on the way from his office.

"No, it's not the Grand Duke of Luxembourg," the girls said.

Before they could pick a dog—DING-DONG!

This time there were two new dogs!

The first stepped up and raised his nose.

"*Hooooowl!* My name's Jerome, and here's the point:
I'm the best darned hound around this joint.
I can sniff a treat from miles away.
I know every smell in the U.S.A.
I'll find your socks and your homework too.
I promise to look out for you."

Then the sleek dog made her pitch.

Arf! Arf! I'm Grace, and I love to race.
I love to jog and keep the pace.
I also like relaxing—all that running can be taxing.
Take me. I'm classy. I won't be sassy."

The girls could hear their mom's footsteps overhead.
"We'll be right back," they whispered to the dogs and
shut the doors.

"Is it the Dalai Lama? I'm not in the right frame of mind for the Dalai Lama," their mom called down. "No, it's not the Dalai Lama," they called back. Before they could decide what to do—DING-DONG! Three more dogs were headed their way . . . The gold-colored one spoke up.

"*Woof! Woof!* My name is Dwight.
No need to check; I'm always right.
I know it all, from A to Z:
From fetch to foreign policy.
I'll be your friend and woo heads of state—
Choose me now, don't hesitate!"

Next, an odd pair came forward, "Excuse me, my name is Lee . . . ," the little puppy began, but he was interrupted by his companion.

"*Grr! Grr! Grr!* My name is Jake.
And let's be frank, I like my steak.
That's why I'm so big and strong.
When I'm around, nothin' goes wrong.
I'm at your service; I can start today.
I'll keep those other dogs away! *Grrr!*"

"Hold your tails! We'll be right back," the older sister said.

"Is it the Emir of Qatar?" their mom asked. She was coming down the stairs. "I'm ready now."

"No, it's not the Emir of Qatar," they said and leaned their backs against the doors.

"Oh, girls! You're not dressed for the party. Hurry upstairs and change!"

The sisters ran past their mom, past the gowns
laid on their beds, straight to the bedroom window.

The dogs were still waiting!

Why did the party have to last so long? First, the parade of handshakes and curtsies. Next, a six-course meal. Then, talk, talk, talk. Would the dogs wait?

"Why do they always have to kiss us on both cheeks?" whispered the older sister, as the last guests finally said good-bye.

"I'd rather be drooled on by a dog," said the younger.

No sooner had she said it than the house filled with barking. The dogs had gotten inside!

The girls dashed from the kitchen to the bedrooms
to the bathroom, catching dogs.
At the door of their dad's office they came to a stop.
There stood their parents.

"Um, we can explain!"

"You've always said we can do anything we . . . *Ha-choo!*
Ha-choo! Ha-choo!"

Everyone jumped at the sneezes . . . except for one puppy,
who edged his way forward.

"Pardon me, my name is Lee.
It's clear you've got an allergy.
I don't wanna brag or boast,
But I've got this fur that's unlike most.
You'll never sneeze with me around;
I learned this fact while at the pound.
A puppy for your family!
Just say you will consider me."

The girls rushed to Lee. "Can we keep him? Please?"
"After all this effort, how could we refuse?" their dad said.
"But what about the other dogs?" the girls asked.
"Well, we can't keep them all, but I have a plan," he said.

New Canine Cabinet Named

(Pictured left to right): Stan (Old English Sheepdog), Jake (Rottweiler), Jerome (Basset Hound), Dwight (Yellow Labrador Retriever), Minnie (Miniature Poodle), Grace (Greyhound)

Organized Dog Hired for Chief of Staff

Tough Dog Hired for Secretary of Defense

Scent-Sniffing Hound Hired for Secretary of Homeland Security

Diplomatic Dog Hired for Secretary of State

Personal Shopper Hired for Secretary of Commerce

Fast Dog Hired for Secretary of Transportation

Tails were wagging all over Washington! All the
dogs had found a home. And one very special puppy
was sworn in as top dog!